P9-DMP-928

E·V·E·R·Y·B·O·D·Y
Makes Mistakes

CHRISTINE KOLE MACLEAN
ILLUSTRATED BY C. B. DECKER

DUTTON CHILDREN'S BOOKS

0 0022 0127734 6

HA CASS COUNTY PUBLIC LIBRARY
400 E. MECHANIC
HARRISONVILLE, MO 64701

Text copyright © 2005 by Christine Kole MacLean

Illustrations copyright © 2005 by C. B. Decker

All rights reserved.

Library of Congress Cataloging-in-Publication Data

MacLean, Christine Kole.

Everybody makes mistakes/by Christine Kole MacLean; illustrated by C. B. Decker.—1st ed.

p.   cm.

Summary: Although he reminds his mother that everybody makes mistakes, and provides a lot of examples,

young Jack is still in hot water for making three big mistakes while playing with his younger sister on their uncle's wedding day.

ISBN 0-525-47225-8

[1. Errors—Fiction. 2. Family life—Fiction. 3. Weddings—Fiction.] I. Decker, C. B., ill. II. Title.

PZ7.M22423Ew   2005   [E]—dc22   2003062614

Published in the United States by Dutton Children's Books, a division of Penguin Young Readers Group

345 Hudson Street, New York, New York 10014

www.penguin.com/youngreaders

Designed by Heather Wood

Manufactured in China

First Edition

1   3   5   7   9   10   8   6   4   2

To my parents, who gave me room to make mistakes,
and Andy, Mary, Bev, Julee, and Margaret, who put up with them
—C.K.M.

To Tutu, where it all started
—C.B.D.

"You are in trouble, Jackson," my mom says. "Big trouble."
All I did was make one little mistake.

Everybody makes
mistakes.

Last winter my mom
forgot to buy me a hat
and mittens to replace
the ones I lost.

So I had to wear my
sister's to school.

"No one will notice,"
Mom told me.

She was wrong.

"Hey, maybe nobody will notice Cammy's new look," I say to my mom.

"Maybe," she says. "If all the guests wear blindfolds."

We all make mistakes sometimes. When I was little, my dad broke the Monster-Be-Gone Mist before he sprayed my room. "Now how are we going to keep the monsters out?" I asked.

"I'll go buy another bottle," he said.
I told him it was already too late.
"You sure have an active imagination," Dad said.

"All I did was have an active imagination," I say to my mom.
"This time it was a little *too* active," she says.

I can think of lots of people who make mistakes. One time a waitress asked me, "And what would you like, young lady?"

My dad made sure she wouldn't make that mistake again.

"Maybe it would help to cut Cammy's hair," I suggest.

"NO!" Cammy yells from the bathroom. "Everyone will think I'm a boy."

"It's too late now," Mom groans. "Why did you have to do it today?"

What's the big deal? It wasn't even a big mistake, like the one Mrs. Morton made when Cammy was born. She brought a truckload of toys for Cammy—and nothing for me.

"Oh dear," she said. "Can you believe at my age I'm still making mistakes? Next time I'll remember."
Mom told me later there wasn't going to be a next time.

"Next time I'll remember not to do it," I say to my mom.

"But this is the only day that Uncle Kevin is marrying Aunt Lola," she says.

"I guess I got a little carried away," I say.

"Yes, you did," she says.

"Still, it was just one little mistake," I say.
"Three," she says. "None of them little."

But none of them were as big as the one Miss Beal made.

"Today, as a special treat, you may bring your snack to circle time," she said. "Let's all be very careful to keep our snacks on our plates."

I very carefully carried my snack to circle time. Then I very carefully put it down next to me. It stayed on my plate the whole time.

Right up until Miss Beal sat down criss-cross-applesauce.

"I'm not the only one who makes mistakes," I say to my mom. "You and Dad and Mrs. Morton and Miss Beal make them. And Cammy makes them all the time."

"I do not! I'm perfect," says Cammy.

"A perfect mess right now," Mom says. "Why couldn't you two just play nicely?"

We *were* playing nicely.

First we played car.

Then we played castle.

Then Cammy said, "When do we get to play what I want to play?"
"What do you want to play?" I asked.

"Beauty shop," she said. "I get to be the customer."

"No way," I said.

Then she yelled, "Mo-om! Jack won't—"

"Okay, okay," I said. "I'll play beauty shop."

"Make my hair look like a fountain," she said.

I couldn't find a hair band, but my gum worked great.

Next Cammy wanted her face painted. I couldn't find the paints, so I used markers.

"Now do my nails," she said.

After I did, she said, "Oooo! I look fabulous." Then she went to show Mom.

Mom didn't think
Cammy looked fabulous.
   "Well, Cammy liked it,"
I said. "She gave me a big tip."
   Mom said, "I have an even bigger tip for you.
NEVER use permanent markers on your sister."

"Ooops," I said. "I guess
I grabbed the wrong ones
out of the drawer."

"Uncle Kevin's wedding is tonight!" she said. "Now what are we going to do?"

"Color her dress so it matches her nails?" I asked.

That's when she sent me to my room. "Jackson!" she said. "You will never watch TV again. And you can just forget about leaving this house until you're eighteen."

"Does that mean I don't have to go to the wedding?"
"*After the wedding* you can just forget about leaving this house until you're eighteen."

On the way to the wedding, Dad says, "Mistakes happen.
Nobody's perfect."
"I am!" says Cammy.

When we get there, Uncle Kevin says, "Wow, Cammy. You look so . . . special!"

"I know," she says. "Jack played beauty shop on me."

"I didn't know that all that stuff wouldn't come off," I say.

"That's okay, Jack. Everybody makes mistakes," he says.

And then my new Aunt Lola whispers, "I can see I'm going to like you."

"I didn't know that all that stuff wouldn't come off," I say.

"That's okay, Jack. Everybody makes mistakes," he says.

And then my new Aunt Lola whispers, "I can see I'm going to like you."

I think I'm going to like her, too.